D0116418

The Thing About Spring

Daniel Kirk

ABRAMS BOOKS FOR YOUNG READERS ❧ NEW YORK

"The world looks a little different today," Mouse said one bright morning.

"It smells different too," said Bird. "There are buds on the trees and new colors in the sky, and I feel warm and happy."

"Me too," said Mouse. "Spring is finally here. Hooray!"

Mouse and Bird hurried to share the good news with their friends. Rabbit was in the meadow, busy with a shovel and pail.

"What are you doing, Rabbit?" Mouse called.

"Saving snow, while I still can," Rabbit grumbled. "We won't see any more of this until next year!"

"But spring is coming," Bird chirped. "Aren't you excited?"

"Excited?" said Rabbit. "Hah! The thing about spring is that I won't be able to follow my friends' tracks in the snow. Then I won't be able to find them!"

"But now you won't be cold," said Bird. "And you won't have to look for me. I'll be right beside you!"

"Me too," said Mouse.

"The thing about spring," said Rabbit, "is that I won't be able to make snow bunnies anymore."

"I won't be able to build snow forts, either. You know how much fun I have doing that!"

"And I won't be able to make snowballs to throw at my favorite targets!"

"But little shoots will grow out of the ground," Mouse said, "so you won't have to look far to find delicious things to eat."

"The thing about spring," said Rabbit, "is that Bear is waking up! You know how bad he smells at the end of a long winter, and I'm sure he's going to want a hug."

"Oh, Rabbit," said Bear with a yawn, "just because I'm a little stinky doesn't mean we can't share a big hug!"

"I want a hug too!" said Bird.

"Me three!" said Mouse.

"The thing about spring," said Rabbit, "is that it rains when you're not expecting it!"

"But rain brings out the flowers," said Mouse.

"And the worms," said Bird.

"And it makes you clean," said Bear, "and ready for more hugs!"

"The thing about spring," said Rabbit, "is that when the days get longer, the nights get shorter—and I am a cranky bunny when I don't get enough sleep!"

"But in the spring, we need more daytime because there are so many things to do!" said Bird.

"In the spring, I love to make loop-de-loops and race the clouds through the sky!" said Bird.

"In the spring, I love to nibble tasty buds and dig tunnels in the soft pine needles," said Mouse.

"In the spring, I love to splash in the lake and dance in the sun," said Bear. "Spring is wonderful!"

"The thing about spring," said Rabbit, "is that all the animals chatter on and on, and the racket hurts my ears!"
"I'll try to be more quiet," whispered Bird.

"Me too," whispered Mouse.

"Me three," whispered Bear, "but it's hard not to make a little noise . . ."

"All right," Rabbit sighed. "I suppose no one can stop the seasons from changing. But the thing about spring is that when I stomp around so much, and the sun is so warm, it makes me really thirsty!"

"Me too," said Bear. "I think we're all a little thirsty!"

"Well, then," said Rabbit, "you should be glad I saved some snow. Look inside my pail! The thing about spring is that it's full of surprises."

"It's wonderful," Bird cheeped.
"Now that spring is here, the snow has
turned to water!"
	"It's like the winter gave us a present
before it went away," said Mouse.

"I found some cups," Rabbit said. "Dip in! It will be our last taste of winter."

"And our first sip of spring," said Bird.

"Here's to spring," said Bear. "I think it's going to be great!"

"Me too," said Bird.

"Me three," said Mouse.

The friends looked at Rabbit.

"Oh, all right," he said. "Me four. Spring is here. Hooray!"

For my friends at the Glen Ridge Library Children's Department:
Jennifer Agarwal, Kathy Hunziker, Joan Lisovicz, and Sydney Young

The illustrations in this book were made with pen and ink,
which were then scanned, and color and texture were added digitally.

Library of Congress Cataloging-in-Publication Data
Kirk, Daniel, author, illustrator.
The thing about spring / Daniel Kirk.
pages cm
Summary: As his friends Bird, Mouse, and Bear celebrate the arrival of spring, Rabbit finds more and more things to
dislike about the change of seasons until, at last, he admits that spring can be full of pleasant surprises.
ISBN 978-1-4197-1492-4 (hardcover)
[1. Spring—Fiction. 2. Seasons—Fiction. 3. Change—Fiction. 4. Animals—Fiction.] I. Title
PZ7.K6339Thi 2015
[E]—dc23
2014016108

Text and illustrations copyright © 2015 Daniel Kirk
Book design by Maria T. Middleton

Printed and bound in China
10 9 8 7 6 5 4 3 2 1

Abrams Books for Young Readers are available at special discounts when purchased in quantity for premiums and
promotions as well as fundraising or educational use. Special editions can also be created to specification. For details,
contact specialsales@abramsbooks.com or the address below.

ABRAMS
THE ART OF BOOKS SINCE 1949
115 West 18th Street
New York, NY 10011
www.abramsbooks.com